# Pete the Cat

## and His Magic Sunglasses

For my mum and dad
Thank you for always being there and believing in me! Phil. 4:11.
—K.D.

For Dorsey and Helen
You are an example to me of what it means
to be a good mum and dad. I am blessed to have you in my life.
—J.D.

First published in hardback by HarperCollins Publishers, USA, in 2013
First published in paperback in Great Britain by HarperCollins Children's Books in 2015

3 5 7 9 10 8 6 4

ISBN: 978-0-00-759078-0

HarperCollins Children's Books is a division of HarperCollins Publishers Ltd.
Copyright © 1999 by James Dean (for the character of Pete the Cat)
Copyright © 2013 by Kimberley and James Dean

Visit our website at www.harpercollins.co.uk
Printed and bound in China

# Pete the Cat

## and His
## Magic Sunglasses

Illustrated by
James Dean

Story by
Kimberly and
James Dean

HarperCollins *Children's Books*

Pete the Cat did not feel happy. Pete had never, ever, ever, ever been grumpy before. Pete had the blue cat blues.

Then, as if things were not bad enough, along came Grumpy Toad. Grumpy Toad was never happy! He always wore a frown.

But Grumpy Toad was not GRUMPY today.
He said, "These COOL, BLUE, MAGIC sunglasses
make the blues go away.

They help you see things in a whole new way."

Pete put on the COOL, BLUE, MAGIC sunglasses.
He looked all around.

"RIGHT ON!

The birds are singing
The sky is bright.
The sun is shining.
I'm feeling ALRIGHT!"

Pete thanked Grumpy Toad for the COOL, BLUE, MAGIC sunglasses. He went on his way, and soon he saw Squirrel. Squirrel did not look happy. Pete said,

"What's wrong, Squirrel?"

Pete said, "Try these COOL, BLUE, MAGIC sunglasses. They help you see things in a whole new way."

Squirrel put on the COOL, BLUE, MAGIC sunglasses and looked all around.

"AWESOME!
The birds are singing.
The sky is bright.
The sun is shining.
I'm feeling ALRIGHT!"

Pete said goodbye to Squirrel and continued on his way. Soon he saw his friend Turtle. Turtle did not look happy.

"What's wrong, turtle?" Pete asked.

# "I'm so FRUSTRATED!

Nothing is going my way. I am all upside down today."

Pete said, "Try these COOL, BLUE, MAGIC sunglasses. They help you see things in a whole new way."

Turtle put on the COOL, BLUE, MAGIC sunglasses and looked all around.

"FAR OUT!
The birds are singing.
The sky is bright.

The sun is shining.
I'm feeling ALRIGHT!"

Pete kept rolling along until he saw Alligator.
Alligator did not look happy.

"What's wrong, Alligator?"
Pete asked.

"I'm so SAD!

Nothing is going my way. No one wants to play with me today."

Pete said, "Try these COOL, BLUE, MAGIC sunglasses. They help you see things in a whole new way."

EASY STREET

Alligator put on the COOL, BLUE, MAGIC sunglasses and looked all around.

"ROCKIN'!

Pete was rolling along and feeling ALRIGHT
when suddenly he fell back.

The COOL, BLUE, MAGIC sunglasses went CRACK. Uh-oh! Pete didn't know what to do without those sunglasses.

Just then, Pete looked up at the tree. Wise Old Owl said, "Pete, you don't need magic sunglasses to see things in a new way. Just remember to look for the good in every day."

Pete looked around without his sunglasses.

"TOO COOL!

The birds are singing.

The sky is bright.

The sun is shining.

# Don't be sad! There's more Pete the Cat to read!

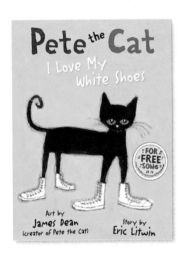

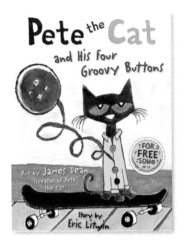

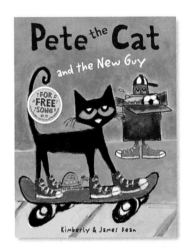

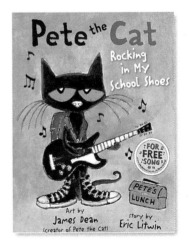